Sam Sheep can't sleep

Russell Punter

Adapted from a story by Phil Roxbee Cox

Illustrated by Stephen Cartwright

Designed by Helen Cooke
Edited by Jenny Tyler and Lesley Sims
Reading consultants: Alison Kelly and Anne Washtell

There is a little yellow duck to find on every page.

Sam Sheep can't sleep.
It's one in the morning.

He turns on the light,
and Pup wakes up, yawning.

"I just don't feel tired.
Pup, what can I do?"

Why not go
for a stroll?

I can tag
along too.

"That's a great plan!" says Sam,
as he pops on his hat.

"I know who might help –
we can chat with Fat Cat."

It is dark in the park.
"There's Fat Cat on his mat."

They go round to Ted's house.
Through a window they peep.

There's Ted in his bed.
But their friend's sound asleep.

They tap on the window.
Ted turns on his light.

"Just what are you up to
at this time of night?"

"How can Sam get some sleep?
We've come to ask you."

They creep through the streets
till they reach Big Pig's place.

Big Pig is awake,
a glum look on her face.

"Sam Sheep can't sleep?
Nor can I," sighs Big Pig.

"But, as we're all here,
let's make space for a jig!"

They wiggle and jiggle
till a quarter past two.

Puzzles

Puzzle 1

Put these animals in the order Sam visited them.

Ted   Big Pig   Fat Cat

Puzzle 2

One word is wrong in this speech bubble. What should it say?

Puzzle 3
Spot the differences between these two pictures.
There are six to find.

Puzzle 4
Who woke up? Who couldn't sleep?

Pup   Sam Sheep   Big Pig   Ted

Answers to puzzles

Puzzle 1

Sam Sheep visited his friends in this order:

1 Fat Cat   2 Ted   3 Big Pig

Puzzle 2

Why not go for a <u>stroll</u>?

Puzzle 3

Puzzle 4

 Pup woke up.

 Sam Sheep couldn't sleep.

 Ted woke up.

 Big Pig couldn't sleep.

About phonics

Phonics is a method of teaching reading used extensively in today's schools. At its heart is an emphasis on identifying the *sounds* of letters, or combinations of letters, that are then put together to make words. These sounds are known as phonemes.

Starting to read

Learning to read is an important milestone for any child. The process can begin well before children start to learn letters and put them together to read words. The sooner children can discover books and enjoy stories and language, the better they will be prepared for reading themselves, first with the help of an adult and then independently.

You can find out more about phonics on the Usborne Very First Reading website, **usborne.com/veryfirstreading** (US readers go to **veryfirstreading.com**). Click on the **Parents** tab at the top of the page, then scroll down and click on **About synthetic phonics**.

Phonemic awareness

An important early stage in pre-reading and early reading is developing phonemic awareness: that is, listening out for the sounds within words. Rhymes, rhyming stories and alliteration are excellent ways of encouraging phonemic awareness.

In this story, your child will soon identify the *ee* sound, as in **sheep** and **sleep**. Look out, too, for rhymes such as **morning** – **yawning** and **light** – **night**.

Hearing your child read

If your child is reading a story to you, don't rush to correct mistakes, but be ready to prompt or guide if he or she is struggling. Above all, give plenty of praise and encouragement.

This edition first published in 2020 by Usborne Publishing Ltd., Usborne House, 83-85 Saffron Hill, London EC1N 8RT, England. usborne.com Copyright © 2020, 2006, 1999 Usborne Publishing Ltd.